GHOST TOWN

TERRY DEARY

ILLUSTRATED BY
CHARLOTTE FIRMIN

Black Cats

The Ramsbottom Rumble • Georgia Byng
Calamity Kate • Terry Deary
Ghost Town • Terry Deary
The Custard Kid • Terry Deary
The Treasure of Crazy Horse • Terry Deary
Dear Ms • Joan Poulson
It's a Tough Life • Jeremy Strong
Big Iggy • Kaye Umansky

First paperback edition 2001
First published in hardback 1992 by
A & C Black (Publishers) Ltd
37 Soho Square, London W1D 3QZ

Text copyright © 1992 Terry Deary
Illustrations copyright © 1992 Charlotte Firmin
Cover illustration copyright © 2001 Michael Terry

ISBN 0-7136-5994-7

A CIP catalogue for this book is available from the
British Library.

Printed and bound in Spain by G. Z. Printek, Bilbao.

Bad News at The Copper Nugget

Sheriff Sam Simple sat in the saloon and sipped a sarsaparilla.

Slowly.

Sheriff Sam Simple did everything slowly these days. He was ninety-two years old and didn't catch too many crooks – only the very stupid ones. Like the bank-robber who broke into a bank and couldn't break out. Or the horse thief who couldn't ride.

Luckily there weren't too many crimes in Deadwood Town. And none at all in The Copper Nugget Saloon where Sam spent most of his time playing cards.

Until . . . one winter's night . . .

The bar-room was crowded. The old piano jangled out an even older tune. A young girl in a blue spotted dress tried to sing – but she didn't know all of the words.

'Home, home on the range,
Where the deer and the tra-la-la play.
Where seldom is heard a dee-dah-dee-dah word,
And the skies are not doo-be-doo day.'

Her name was Calamity Kate and she had sung in all the bars in Dakota state trying to make a bit of money.

Suddenly the door swung open. An angry voice cried out, 'Will you shut that door! Per-lease! It's cold in here.'

The door swung shut. Young Josiah Hepgutt, who was only eighty-two, staggered to the bar and gasped, 'Give me a shot of red-eye whisky!'

His wife, Martha, stood behind the bar and glared at him. 'Say "please".' She was sharper than a sewing-box full of needles.

'Ohh, *please* give me a big shot of red-eye whisky,' the young eighty-two year old groaned.

Martha gave him a glass of milk and snapped, 'Sit down before you fall down, you silly old buzzard.'

Josiah hauled himself on to a bar stool, sipped the milk and turned to the sheriff. 'Sam!' he croaked. 'Trouble!'

The sheriff leapt to his feet faster than a sleepy snail and staggered over to Josiah.

'Eh?' he said and cupped a hand around his ear.

Josiah yelled so loud that the whole bar-room went silent. 'I said TROUBLE!'

Even the piano-player stopped playing. Calamity Kate, who didn't know the words, stopped singing. Even the flies stopped flying. Only the cold wind whistled through the broken window pane – perhaps it whistled because it didn't know the words either.

Now that everyone was looking at Josiah he felt a little foolish. 'Er . . . ah . . . oh . . .'

'Spit it out, old timer,' a shabby cowboy cried.

Josiah cleared his throat. 'I've just come back from Flatfoot Town,' he said.

'Nice place, Flatfoot,' Calamity Kate said cheerfully. Kate always tried to be cheerful.

'Yep,' Josiah agreed. He peered at her pretty, freckled face and smiled a toothless smile. 'Took my old horse in for a check-up.'

'Yeah? What was the problem? No tread left on the hooves?' asked Kate.

'Nope,' Josiah replied. 'Loose nosebag!'

'Oh, my! That's terrible,' Kate tutted and shook her red-haired head sadly.

The shabby cowboy sighed a long, loud sigh. 'Just get on with the story, old timer.'

That upset Martha Hepgutt who was polishing glasses behind the bar. After she had polished them she put them back on the end of her nose. 'Kindly refrain from calling my husband an old timer. He isn't a grandfather clock, you know!'

The cowboy sneered. 'Anybody ever tell you that you squawk like an old crow?'

Martha's eyes narrowed. She leaned forward. 'Yep!'

The shabby cowboy blinked. 'And?'

'And he never got served in this saloon again,' Martha said quietly. The cowboy looked into his glass uncomfortably and sniffed. Martha gave a sharp nod and said, 'So, get on with the story, Josiah.'

'Well,' Josiah began. 'This loose nosebag has been bothering me for some time and . . . '

'The *story*,' Martha cried.

'Sorry, Martha,' the young eighty-two year old mumbled and took a sip of his milk. 'I called into The Crying Shame Saloon for a glass of red-eye . . . '

'You did what?' Martha said and her voice crackled dangerously.

'Er . . . a glass of *milk* dear,' Josiah said, smiling weakly at Martha. 'But when I got to the saloon it was wrecked.'

'Wrecked!' everyone gasped.

'No one would wreck a *saloon!*' the shabby cowboy argued.

Josiah fixed him with a watery eye and said quietly, 'Big Bart would.'

Sheriff Sam Simple cupped a hand to his ear. 'A bit of hard wood, did you say?'

'No,' Calamity Kate explained gently. 'Big Bart. I heard about him last time I was in Flatfoot Town. According to the people of Flatfoot, he's a terrible villain. When he loses his temper he can wreck any place.'

'But a saloon,' the shabby cowboy moaned. 'Nobody wrecks a *saloon*.'

'That's what they said when they threw him out of town,' Josiah nodded. 'Told him if he wanted to wreck a saloon he should go to Deadwood.'

'He's coming *here*!' Martha Hepgutt screeched. 'He'd better not try to wreck this saloon.'

'You couldn't stop him,' Josiah said.

'No,' Martha admitted. 'But Sheriff Sam Simple could!'

Everyone turned to look at the sheriff. He twisted his stained, grey moustache nervously. 'Sorry, folks, I have to get home and take a bath.'

'Bath!' Martha cried. 'You haven't had a bath in winter in the twenty years I've known you.'

'Well . . . it's time I did,' the sheriff sniffed and shuffled towards the door. But before he could reach it, the door crashed open.

'Will you shut that door! Per-lease! It's cold in here,' the angry voice called.

The door stayed open. Yet there was no draught. The man who stood there filled the entire door frame.

He was wide – but not much wider than a stagecoach. He was tall – but not much taller than a telegraph pole.

'Give me a large shot of red-eye,' he said in a rumbling voice that set the flies buzzing again.

'Say please,' Martha snapped at the stranger.

'P-p-please give me a large shot of red-eye,' the huge man babbled.

Martha poured the drink. Josiah's shaking hand carried it to the giant of a man. He swallowed it in one gulp and gasped. 'I needed that,' he croaked. 'I've just heard some terrible news . . . '

This time even the wind stopped whistling to listen.

The man's eyes bulged with fear as he told the hushed saloon, 'I've just heard . . . Big Bart is coming to town!'

But . . .

2

Big Bart Hits Town

. . . Big Bart was still a long way from Deadwood Town. And Big Bart was boiling mad. Big Bart's bad temper was bubbling.

'Banned from the bar!' he sniffled as he stomped along the dusty road to Deadwood Town. 'Big Bart banned from the bar because he broke a measly beer bottle!'

But the truth was that the beer bottle he had broken had been on a shelf . . . and Bart had broken it by throwing a bar-stool at it. The stool had broken the mirror behind the bar and most of the glasses in The Crying Shame Saloon. As if that wasn't enough he then called the barman 'a ferret-faced fool' and refused to pay for the damage.

'Get out, and don't come back,' the barman told him. And everyone in The Crying Shame Saloon cheered. They were fed up with Big Bart's bad behaviour.

'Nobody likes me,' he snarled as he headed for the door. 'And I don't like nobody. I'm leaving this town for good.' He packed a bag and by sunset was heading down the main street. The cheers followed behind him.

Big Bart's breath steamed in the cold night air

and his feet stumbled on the stony road. Every stone seemed set to trip him up. The night was dark. Lonely coyotes howled a haunting tune in the hills. They didn't seem to know the words either.

At last Bart reached a fork in the road. A sign post pointed in three directions. 'Flatfoot Town 5' it said for the road Bart had just come along.

The right-hand path said 'Deadwood Town 4'. Big Bart studied it in the faint starlight. 'Hmm. Four, eh?'

The pointer to the left said 'Ghost Town 3'.

'Hmm. Three, eh? That's not so far.'

Big Bart had never learned to read words – only numbers. He set off along the left-hand trail for Ghost Town.

It was a steep mountain trail that climbed into the hills. A narrow, weed-covered trail that was never used these days. And a silent, lonely trail that even the owls and the coyotes avoided.

The three miles seemed like thirty to the tired Bart. His light bag felt like lead. At last he reached the town sign and leaned against it. If he had been able to read he'd have known it said, 'Ghost Town – Population 000'.

A thin wind chilled him and ruffled the weeds in the street. Old signs creaked softly as they swung back and forth. Bart shivered and spoke out loud to comfort himself.

'Always heard that Deadwood was a bit livelier than this. Hah!'

'Hah!' came an echo from the shadows.

Big Bart swung round and squinted into the dark corner by a deserted barber's shop.

'Is there anybody there?'

'Where?' came the reply.

'There!'

'Here?'

'There!'

'Yeah!'

'Then come out where I can see you,' Bart snapped and his bad temper began to rise – he hated people making fun of him. From the shadows stepped the thinnest man he'd ever seen. So thin Bart thought he could see straight past him – almost straight *through* him – to the barber shop behind.

But the thin man looked friendly enough. A faint grin lit his pale face as he walked towards Bart.

'I'm Big Bart,' Bart said boldly.

'Seems I've heard that name before,' the thin man smiled.

Bart blushed. 'I *am* quite famous,' he admitted.

'But not as famous as my brother and I,' the stranger said softly.

Bart stared at the face but it seemed hard to focus on the faint features. 'I've never seen your face on a wanted poster,' he sniffed.

'No. But you've heard of Billy the Kid?'

Bart gasped. 'Billy the Kid died forty years ago!'

The stranger just nodded. 'My brother,' he explained. 'And perhaps you've heard of me . . . I'm Sid the Kid.'

Bart frowned. 'The famous train robber? I thought Sid the Kid died long ago too, killed by a runaway train.'

'Is that what they say?' the stranger chuckled. 'Don't believe everything you hear.'

Bart shivered again as the breeze swept down the single street of Ghost Town. 'Can you tell me the way to The Copper Nugget Saloon?' Bart asked.

'Saloon's over here,' Sid the Kid said with a nod of his head. 'Let me show you.'

He led the way to some old wooden steps and let Bart walk past him to a warped wooden door. Bart pushed hard. The door flew open . . . and something flew out. Something furry and fierce and spitting. Bart yelped in horror.

Sid the Kid laughed. 'Nothing but an old cat.'

The cat arched its back and gave a low growl as it stared at Sid the Kid. The thin train-robber chuckled and growled back. The startled cat shot off into the shadows down the street. Bart shuddered and moaned, 'If there's one thing I can't stand it's cats. I'd rather face a grizzly bear than a cat any day.'

Sid shrugged and led the way into the dim room. 'No grizzly bears in here,' he said, turning up an oil lamp that hung from the ceiling. 'This saloon's been empty for ages . . . it's a quiet kind of place, except of course at midnight,' he sniggered.

Bart looked around. Dust lay thick on the tables. Cobwebs dangled from the bar and smothered the bottles.

If Bart had been a little brighter he might have noticed the dust that was thick on the floor. For, as Sid the Kid led the way across to the stairs, the thin cowboy left no footprints in the dust. The only footprints were those of the cat and of some very small boots with a high heel.

Big Bart noticed none of this as he followed Sid the Kid up the stairs. And he didn't notice that his feet creaked on the crumbling stairs while Sid's were silent.

The train robber reached the door to a room and turned towards Bart. 'This one's free,' he grinned.

'Good,' Bart grunted. 'I don't have much money at the moment.'

Sid the Kid lit a lamp on the bedside table. It cast shadows round the dingy room . . . but Sid's pale body cast no shadows. The sly grin slid over his face again. 'Not much money, eh?'

'Not a bean,' Big Bart admitted.

'Not a cent?'

'Not a button.'

Sid the Kid leaned closer to Big Bart and whispered in his creaking voice, 'Then I think I have a plan. A plan that could make us both richer than a freight-train full of fifty-dollar bills.'

'Fifty-dollar bills? I've never seen one of those,' Big Bart breathed.

'Interested?'

Bart sank on to the edge of the broken bed and nodded slowly. 'Interested!' Even the spiders in the Ghost Town saloon listened . . .

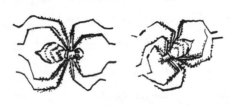

3

Calamity Kate's Cat

. . . while in Deadwood Town, The Copper Nugget Saloon was quiet. The cowards had crept home to bed when they'd heard that Big Bart was on his way into town. The rest were curious but quiet as they huddled at the tables. The piano was silent and Calamity Kate had sung all the songs that she didn't know.

'Doesn't look like he's going to make it,' Martha Hepgutt said at last. 'May as well close the place. Drink up, folks!'

'He could be out there, somewhere in the dark – waiting!' Josiah Hepgutt hissed.

'Oooh! You think so?' Calamity Kate asked.

'Josiah!' Martha snapped. 'Can't you see you're scaring the girl?' She turned to the young singer. 'You got far to go home, Miss Kate?'

'Oh, just up the hill – quiet little place,' said Kate.

'Hmm, what's it called?'

'Ghost Town,' Kate told Martha brightly. 'Funny kind of name, isn't it?'

And suddenly it seemed that everyone in the bar was looking at her. 'Ghost Town?' the shabby cowboy gasped. 'Nobody in their right mind would live in Ghost Town.'

Kate shrugged. 'Sid the Kid does. Nice man. He lets me have a room in the old saloon for next to nothing.'

'I think someone should see this little lady safely back to her home,' Martha Hepgutt said quickly. 'Bad enough living in Ghost Town, but with Big Bart on the loose *nobody* should be out alone. How about you taking Miss Kate home?' she said sharply to the shabby cowboy.

'Sorry. I live at the other side of town,' he muttered and slithered out of the door like a well-oiled worm.

'Josiah?' Martha snapped.

'I have to see you home, my love . . . and, anyway, I don't have a gun. Why not ask Sam Simple? He is the sheriff, after all.'

Martha sighed. 'He's about as much use as a bald paintbrush. Still, there doesn't seem to be a lot of choice,' she said looking round at the remaining cowboys. 'Sam!' she called. 'See this young lady home.'

'Eh?' the sheriff asked and cupped a hand to his ear. 'Write this lady a poem? Very well . . .'

You're fair as a rose on a bright summer's day;
You sing twice as sweet as the birds.
You'd be the best singer in all the wild west
If only you knew all the words!

Martha buried her face in her hands. 'Sam!' she shouted. 'Take Miss Kate HOME to Ghost Town!'

'Ghost Town!' he croaked. 'Nobody goes to Ghost Town after dark.'

'Are you a man or a mouse?' Martha roared.

Sam Simple thought about this for a minute. Finally he answered. 'Yes.'

Kate skipped over to the old man and linked an arm through his. 'Don't worry, Mr Simple,' she smiled. 'I'll look after you.'

And the curious couple set off into the frost-bright night. Kate chatted happily and Sam Simple panted miserably as they climbed towards the hilltop town. 'Why do they call it Ghost Town?' Kate asked, directing her question at Sam's right ear.

Sam gasped like a drowning goldfish and sat down on a boulder to catch his breath. 'Nothing to do with ghosts, of course,' he managed to say. 'Just the name people give to any deserted town.'

'But where did all the people go?' Kate asked.

'Oh, they built the town there when there was gold in these hills. When the gold ran out the people moved down to Deadwood Town in the valley. The stagecoach runs along the valley and the railroad came to Deadwood soon after, so there wasn't any point living up in the hills any more.'

Kate sat next to the old man and nodded. 'So why does Sid the Kid still live there? He found me a room at the saloon with no name,' she said.

The old man's eyes rolled fearfully. 'Sid the Kid died forty years ago!' he said.

Kate laughed and her voice echoed round the rocks. 'Didn't look too dead to me. Maybe this is the son of Sid the Kid – Sid the Kid's kid,' she suggested.

'Or maybe he's a g-g-g- . . . ' Sam Simple gargled and couldn't bring himself to say the word.

'A what?'

'Er . . . a g-grandson of Sid the train-robbing Kid,' the sheriff said weakly.

'Maybe, and perhaps he *likes* living up here all alone,' said Kate. 'Still, whoever he is, he's very pleasant to me. Very polite.'

'That's good,' Sheriff Sam Simple said as he rose to his feet and hurried on along the path like a tortoise treading through treacle . . . which was twice as fast as usual.

At last they reached the top of the ridge and looked back at the town of Deadwood which glowed warmly in the valley. The main street of Ghost Town stretched out silently. Not an owl hooted and not a dog barked. But in the soft rustling of the weeds Kate heard a tiny sound and felt a gentle rub against her high-heeled boot.

She stooped down and swept up the animal. 'Hey! Sheriff! It's Tiger!' Kate said softly. Too softly.

The old man's hand fluttered by his side and pulled out his rusty pistol. 'A tiger? Where? Don't worry, Miss Kate, I'll shoot it for you.' He crouched low and pointed his gun at the shadows. 'Never seen a tiger in Deadwood,' he whispered. 'Must have escaped from a travelling circus.'

Kate tapped him on the shoulder. 'Wah!' the old man cried. 'It's got me! It's got me!'

Kate calmly held the cat in front of Sam Simple's nose. 'Cat!' she said simply. 'My cat!'

'A rat?' the old man cried and pointed his gun at it. 'Put it down before it bites you,' he advised.

'It's a cat,' Kate said slowly and spelled it for the sheriff. 'C-A-T.'

'Did it kill the tiger?' he asked, confused.

'No. Tiger is his name,' she went on patiently.

'Tiger has a mane?' Sam gasped. 'Think you're wrong there, Miss Kate. Tigers don't have manes. Lions have manes. You reckon there's a lion loose?' he gibbered.

Kate gave up trying to explain but as she put the cat down a worrying thought crossed her mind. How had Tiger got out? She had left him locked in the saloon. No one could have let him out . . . except Sid the Kid, but he only seemed to appear once a week to collect the rent. Perhaps Tiger had run out when *someone else* went in.

Kate shuddered and turned to the sheriff, 'Mr Simple, I think I know where Big Bart must be,' she whispered fearfully. 'Listen carefully. I am going into the saloon. I want *you* to get back to Deadwood as fast as you can. Fetch a posse!'

'What was that?' the startled sheriff said.

'Fetch the posse!' Kate repeated and tiptoed towards the saloon, where . . .

4

Sid the Kid's Perfect Plan

. . . Sid the Kid was telling Big Bart of his perfectly brilliant plan to rob the Deadwood Express Train.

And Big Bart was listening so carefully he didn't hear the girl creep upstairs to her room next door. She pressed her ear against the thin wooden walls and her red hair turned curlier as she heard the wicked plan.

'So, let's run through that again,' Sid the Kid was saying.

'I understood first time,' Bart said in a slightly huffed voice.

'But I didn't,' Kate murmured to herself.

'First we take the gunpowder,' Sid the Kid said slowly.

'First we take the gunpowder,' Big Bart sighed.

'From the old store,' Sid explained.

'What's it doing there anyway?' Bart asked.

'Miners used to use it to blast the rocks away to find the gold,' the thin villain told him. 'The store still has barrels full of it.'

'So why haven't you used it for this plan before?' Bart asked, suspiciously.

'Never had the strength to carry it down to Deadwood,' Sid said. 'Need a strong pair of arms like yours.'

'Yeah,' Bart said proudly.

'We take the gunpowder down to Deadwood,' Sid went on.

'To Deadwood,' Bart echoed.

'To Deadwood!' Kate squeaked almost too loud.

'And we wait for the mail train.'

'The mail train.'

'And then?'

'Then,' continued Sid a little exasperated, 'I'll uncouple the bank carriage.'

'Surely someone will see you,' protested Bart.

Sid the Kid gave his low chuckle. 'No one EVER sees me unless I want to be seen. Now. Let's get on with the plan.'

'The plan.'

'I take the brake off the carriage and let it roll

back to Sagebush Junction where we won't be disturbed.'

' . . . won't be disturbed.'

'You crawl under the carriage with the barrel . . .'

'Somebody's bound to see me,' Bart argued.

'The mail train comes in just before dawn. No one will see you in the dark, underneath the train.'

'Oh,' said Bart, not sure whether to believe Sid.

'You light the fuse . . . '

'You light the fuse . . . '

'No! *You* light the fuse you fool!'

'No! *I* light the fuse – me fool!'

'And then . . . '

'And then . . . '

Bang! *Bang*! BANG!

Calamity Kate jumped as she heard her name called out in the street below. It was Sheriff Sam Simple hammering at the door.

'What was that?' Big Bart asked.

'Just some shutters slamming in the wind,' Sid the Kid chuckled. 'Don't get nervous.'

Next door, Kate wasn't nervous, she was terrified. 'Oh, no!' she moaned. 'The sheriff hasn't had time to get back to Deadwood and fetch a posse. He must be alone . . . they'll kill me,' she whimpered. The knocking was repeated. Suddenly a new thought struck her. 'Worse! They'll kill *him*!' And that made her very angry – too angry to remember her own fear.

She hurried to the door and tiptoed down the creaking stairs muttering fiercely, 'If they harm a hair of that poor old man's head I'll flatten them flatter than a tomato on a train track!'

Kate tugged at the door and saw the old sheriff standing there, grinning. 'You were quick!' she whispered as loud as she dared.

'No flies on old Sam Simple,' he said happily.

'You got all the way to Deadwood and back in *ten* minutes?' she asked.

'Didn't have to go to Deadwood,' he cackled.

'No? You didn't go to Deadwood? But you got them, didn't you?' Kate said and peered out into the street for some sign of the posse.

'I got it all right – but I didn't have to go to Deadwood! It was just down the main street, under the horse trough.'

'Under the *horse* trough!' Kate gasped.

'That's right, Miss Kate. Hiding. Probably looking for rats,' the sheriff guessed.

'Rats? The posse was out hunting rats? Where is it now?' Kate asked.

The old sheriff's face broke into a huge smile, so big that even his drooping moustache turned up. 'I have it right here,' he said and held up a striped cat that answered to the name of Tiger.

Calamity Kate's mouth fell open. She counted slowly to three to stop herself from screaming, then said clearly, 'The posse, Sheriff – a gang of your deputies – a posse. Not a PUSSY!'

Sam's smile slid slowly off his moustache. 'Oh,' was all he managed to say.

Tiger jumped from his arms and scurried back down the street.

Kate cupped her hands over her mouth and spoke loudly into Sam Simple's ear. 'There are two men in the saloon. They're planning to rob the mail train. Go back to Deadwood and warn everyone.'

Sam nodded. 'Come on then, Miss Kate,' he said.

Kate shook her head. 'I'm going back in there to see if I can learn anything else. I'll catch up with you in ten minutes.'

Sam blinked. 'Miss Kate . . . you could be killed.'

Kate raised her eyes to the dim stars and sighed, 'A girl's gotta do what a girl's gotta do. My ma always said you can kill two birds of a feather with a bird in the bush.'

Sam scratched his head. 'What does that mean, Miss Kate?'

'I never asked her,' Kate admitted. 'But it's very clever and I've never forgotten it.'

'Hah!' the sheriff snorted. 'My old pa always said that fried eggs tell no lies.'

'And what does that mean?' Kate asked.

Sam leaned forward and fixed the girl with his watery eyes. 'It means that if these villains catch you they'll kill you. Maybe I should go and listen to their plans.'

'You'd never hear them – not unless they shouted out loud specially for you – and they're not likely to do that,' she told him.

'Eh?'

'Oh never mind. Just get back to town and warn everyone,' she said as she headed back into the dusty saloon to listen to the two men who were . . .

5

Big Bart's Bad Boyhood

. . . talking about Big Bart's boyhood.

'It was tough,' he was telling Sid the Kid. 'Especially for a kid my size.'

'Guess it must have been,' Sid agreed.

Kate paused in the passageway and decided that she could hear better if she crouched at the door to the room. Lamplight spilled through big cracks in the twisted old door and she pressed her eye to one of them. It was all she could do to keep from crying out loud when she saw the two men.

The thin, pale one seemed to float round the room like a fine net curtain in a breeze. It was the man who let her have the room. 'The other kids picked on you, did they?' he was saying.

'They did,' Big Bart whined . . . and he was even more surprising than Sid the Kid. He stood at the end of the bed – and Kate reckoned that the top of Big Bart's head came about up to her elbow. The terrible Big Bart was tiny. 'They called me "Big" Bart because I was so small – their idea of a joke, I suppose,' he explained to Sid the Kid.

'Didn't your ma and pa stick up for you?' the thin thief asked.

Bart's little face creased into a bitter scowl. 'Never had a ma and pa . . . I was brought up in the orphanage,' he muttered.

'What happened to your parents?' Sid asked.

'Seems they went out into the hills one day – for a picnic – and they were never seen again. Could have been a bear or a mountain lion took them. Or they could have just run away and left me. An old gold miner found me crawling around in the rocks. I was about one year old at the time, they say.'

'That's tough,' Sid admitted.

'I told you that,' Bart sniffed. 'Never had anything but bad luck all my life,' he snarled.

Sid gave his sly smile and said, 'Well, Bart, your luck changed from the moment you met me. I'll make you rich . . . '

'Rich,' Bart echoed.

'And famous.'

'Famous,' Bart crooned and licked his lips at the thought.

'We'll pull off the greatest train robbery ever – you'll go down in history like my brother, Billy the Kid,' Sid promised. 'In a week you'll be the most wanted man in the United States of America.'

Big Bart frowned a little frown. 'Is that good?'

'Good? It's the greatest,' Sid said. His eyes glowed wickedly, almost red. His voice was smooth as a snake's hiss as he said, 'They'll never call you Big Bart again – probably call you *Bad* Bart. They'll never pick on you again. They'll respect you in every saloon in the west.'

'But the law . . . ' Bart muttered.

'The law won't catch you,' Sid promised. 'Not with me to look after you. I have powers that no law man could ever match.'

'What are they?' Bart asked.

'You'll see, you'll see,' Sid smirked and Kate hated him for it. Her legs ached as she crouched at the crack in the door. She shifted her weight slightly and the floorboard creaked softly.

To Kate's horror the two men in the room turned and looked towards the door. She could have sworn that Sid the Kid was looking straight through the door and deep into her frightened eyes. She stepped back carefully and tiptoed towards the stairway.

She looked over her shoulder. The door was still closed. They weren't coming after her. She let out a soft whistle of relief, turned towards the safety of the stairs . . . and screamed.

The pale-grey, red-eyed face of Sid the Kid was grinning at her from the top stair. Kate rushed towards him and pushed past without feeling him try to stop her.

But a wickedly wide crack in a stair caught the heel of her boot. She stumbled, fell forward and tumbled down the dusty stairs from top to bottom . . .

*   *   *

. . . as Sam Simple stumbled and panted into The Copper Nugget Saloon in Deadwood Town.

The saloon was closed, but Martha Hepgutt was sweeping the floor and humming to herself. She looked up and frowned at Sheriff Sam Simple. 'Oh, Sam, it's much too far to Ghost Town for an old man like you – I shouldn't have made you go. Should have made that girl stay here the night.'

'Drains!' Sam gasped.

Martha sniffed. 'Drains? Can't smell no drains. Not since the town council had new ones dug last year.' She leaned on her broom and smiled proudly. 'Deadwood Town has the best drains in the west – and they don't smell,' she added.

'Robbery,' the old man said in a strangled voice as he collapsed into a bar-room chair.

Martha poured a glass of sarsaparilla and passed it to him. 'Robbery? I guess that night air has blown your brains clean away. Haven't had a robbery in Deadwood for twenty years or more. Drink your sarsaparilla and calm down.'

The sheriff took a gulp and wiped his moustache. 'Drain robbery!' he managed to say.

'Drain robbery,' Martha said slowly. 'Are you saying there's going to be a drain robbery? Hmm! Flatfoot Town have always been jealous of our drains, but they wouldn't stoop so low as to steal them. Anyway – how do you steal a drain?'

'Big Bart!' Sam babbled.

'Big Bart's coming to steal our drains? Say! That story about him coming to Deadwood was just phooey! He never showed up.'

'Ghost Town – he's in Ghost Town with Sid the Kid!' Sam said tiredly.

'But where is Miss Kate?' Martha asked, looking round anxiously. 'You haven't left her in Ghost Town?'

'Went back. To hear more about their plans for the drain robbery,' the sheriff explained and drained the sarsaparilla.

'Ohh!' cried Martha. 'What a heroine.'

'Said she'd follow me down in ten minutes,' Sam went on.

'Yeh?' the old woman said waving her broom around like a sword. 'Well we can start our plans now. Those villains want drains? We'll give them drains. Take those table-cloths, Sam, and follow me!' she cried. Hurriedly she led the way into the main street of Deadwood Town eager to set about her plan for the defence of the Deadwood drains against . . .

6

The Drains of Deadwood

. . . Bad Bart and Sid the Kid, who at that precise moment, were busy tying Kate to the post at the foot of the stairs in the saloon with no name. She was knocked out cold – colder than a trout in a mountain stream.

Sid the Kid chuckled nastily as he rummaged through Kate's purse and found two silver dollars and a few cents.

Bart looked troubled. 'No need for that, Sid. By dawn we'll be the richest men in America!'

'She owes me a week's rent,' Sid sneered nastily. 'And if you want to be a famous robber you have to be ready to rob your own ma of her last matchstick.'

'I don't have a ma,' Big Bart muttered miserably. Sid the Kid held out one of the silver dollars to the little man who just shook his head. Sid shrugged.

'Right, *Bad* Bart . . . let's go down to the old store and fetch that barrel of gunpowder,' Sid said as he led the way into the dark street. Bart brought a lantern from the saloon and shivered as he heard the soft growling of a cat in the shadows.

The old store was as rickety as the saloon and the door creaked on its broken hinges as Bart pushed his way in. Sacks of food lay empty on the floor, long since raided by rats. Cans rusted on the shelves and faded clothes hung dusty on their rails. Clothes that had been out of fashion for forty years – clothes that looked exactly like Sid the Kid's.

The tall, thin thief pointed to a barrel in the corner. 'There it is, Bart – a barrel of gunpowder. Enough in there to blow up twenty trains.'

'I'll never carry that,' Bart moaned. 'Not all the way to Deadwood on my little legs.'

'It's only a mile and it's downhill all the way,' Sid sneered. 'Anyway . . . you *roll* the barrel. Didn't they teach you anything at school?'

'Never went to school,' Bart told him as he tipped the barrel on its side.

It rolled across the floor quite easily but Bart panted as he pushed it down the weed-choked street. 'Aren't you going to help?' he asked Sid.

The tall man shrugged. 'I'm the brains of this gang – you're the muscle. Keep pushing.'

So Bart sweated and struggled down the dusty road to Deadwood, unaware that there was quite a welcome waiting for him . . .

*   *   *

. . . on the main street of Deadwood Town. The lanterns flickered yellow and orange. It was bright as day and deserted as a school on Sunday – except for an old man who stood in the middle of the main street on the edge of a table-cloth.

Sheriff Sam Simple fidgeted with his gun and tried to look tough. From the shadows of a shop doorway Martha Hepgutt called to him, 'Now you have a few minutes to practise, Sam. Pretend that Big Bart has just appeared at the other end of the street. What are you going to say?'

'Er . . .' Sam cleared his throat and narrowed his eyes. 'This town ain't big enough for a toothbrush,' he snarled.

37

'No, no, NO!' Martha moaned. 'For the TWO OF US – not for a toothbrush.'

'Sorry Martha, must have misheard you,' Sam grinned. He was tired and cold but this was more fun than he'd had in ten years. 'Er . . . this town ain't big enough for two of us to have a toothbrush.'

Martha shrugged. It didn't matter. With any luck the Deadwood drains would defeat this Bart fellow if Sheriff Sam Simple didn't.

'Tell him about the fight,' Martha advised.

'Oh, yeah,' Sam smiled and stared down the street to where he imagined Big Bart would be standing. 'If you want to take our drains you'll have to eat cat meat first.'

'No, Sam. You'll have to GET PAST ME first,' Martha said with a shake of her head.

'Here he comes, now, Martha!' Sam squeaked and suddenly it seemed a lot less fun. He peered down the street to where Big Bart rolled into town from . . .

* * *

. . . Ghost Town. Calamity Kate stirred and groaned. She shook her head. It hurt. She tried to raise a hand to rub it but found that she was tied to the post at the foot of the stairs in the saloon with no name.

'The good-for-nothing, toad-faced skunks!' she roared and pulled at the rope. The rope was strong.

But the post at the foot of the stairs was rotten. As she pulled she heard it creak. She pushed back hard and heard a crack. Slowly Kate began to pull forward then lean back in a rocking motion, singing in time to her rocking.

'Home, home on the range,
Where the deer and the antelope play
Where seldom is heard, a discouraging word . . .
I've remembered the right words today!'

Kate could see her purse lying on the cobwebbed floor. It was open and empty. 'I've been robbed!' she screamed and gave a final angry tug. The post was ripped loose and Kate was free.

Without the post the banisters slowly collapsed and crashed to the floor.

Without the banister the stairs began to fall down into the bar-room at the bottom. Kate backed towards the door and gaped at the wreckage.

Without the stairs to hold it up the top landing fell down in a cloud of dust and angry spiders.

'Calamity Kate by name and . . . ' the top floor began to join the landing in the avalanche of rotten wood . . . 'Calamity Kate by nature,' the girl muttered as she backed into the street. Just in time.

Without the top floor the ceiling and then the roof fell in. Kate stumbled down the dark street, hands still tied behind her, as the saloon with no name became the saloon with no nothing.

Without the saloon to prop them up the buildings on either side fell over with a roar.

Tiger the cat ran after the fleeing Kate as Ghost Town fell down like a row of drunken dominoes.

Calamity Kate stopped at the sign that said 'Ghost Town – Population 000', looked back and shook her head. 'Sorry, Mr Sid, but I guess my two dollars will have to go towards your new saloon.'

Leaving behind her what was left of the town, Kate stumbled down the dark road till she reached a rough boulder. She bent down and let the rope rest against a sharp edge of the rock.

After ten minutes sawing the rope snapped and Kate was free. She picked up Tiger and rubbed the spot between his ears the way he liked it. 'Better get back to Deadwood Town . . . I don't know how long I was out cold, but I reckon there might still be time to save that mail train.'

Leaving behind the ghost of what was once a town Kate set off for Deadwood where . . .

7

Duel at High Midnight

. . . Sheriff Sam Simple stood waiting for the drain robber.

'Looks like he's rolling someone along!' he gasped.

Martha stepped out into the street and stood alongside the sheriff even though that was not part of the plan. 'No, Sam, he's rolling a barrel. Looks like the sort of barrel they used to keep gunpowder in up in Ghost Town.'

'Ger-ger-gunpowder?' Sam gasped. 'They ain't going to *steal* the drains – they're planning to blow them up!'

'You could be right, Sam. Those Flatfoot Town people must be really jealous of our drains to stoop this low. But a barrel that big would blow up the whole town!'

'Oooh!' Sam wailed. 'What do I do, Martha?'

'Stay calm and go ahead with the plan,' she said.

'C-c-can't remember my words,' Sam stammered.

'I'll stay here and help you,' Martha promised and the odd couple turned to face the man who'd come to wreck their town . . . or so they thought.

Twenty paces away from the sheriff Bart stopped and rubbed his aching back. 'Good morning,

Sheriff,' he said politely. 'You're out late.'

'You're out early,' Martha snapped back. 'Where would you be going at this time of day?'

'Going to catch the early morning train to New York,' Bart said – and that was almost true.

'With a barrel of gunpowder?' the old woman asked and looked down her pointed nose at the little man.

He shrugged and wondered where Sid the Kid had disappeared to when he needed him most. 'Thought I might do a bit of mining,' he said.

'Not a lot of mines in New York, they tell me,' Martha said coldly.

Bart giggled. 'Will be by the time I've finished.'

Martha turned to Sam Simple. 'Tell him to get back to where he came from, Sam.'

Sam cleared his throat. 'This town ain't big enough for your toothbrush!' Sam stuttered.

'Ain't got a toothbrush!' Bart jeered. 'Never clean my teeth.'

Martha looked horrified, 'That's disgusting,' she said. 'Didn't your mother ever make you clean your teeth?'

'Ain't got a mother,' Bart growled.

Martha softened. 'That's sad. I apologise.'

'Apology accepted,' the little man replied.

Sam remembered his next line, 'If you want to get to the drains you'll have to get cat meat first!'

Bart was puzzled but tried to make a sensible reply. 'Don't need cat meat. Don't have a cat. Hate the things!'

'Oh,' Sam muttered. 'What do I do now, Martha?'

'Challenge him to a fight,' she reminded him.

'I challenge you to a fight!' he called.

'To a fight?'

'Yep! Tonight!'

Bart pulled at the strands of curly hair that strayed out from under his hat. Where was Sid the Kid? Dealing with this old nutter wasn't part of the plan. And he didn't want to hurt the old man.

'Guns at thirty paces,' Martha prompted.

'Heh! Gonna give you a dirty face!' the sheriff cried.

Martha bellowed at him, 'Shut up, you dummy.'

Sam heard that. 'Shut up, you dummy,' he shouted to the baffled Bart.

'I never said nothing,' Bart protested.

'I'll do the talking,' Martha said firmly enough for them both to hear. 'Now listen here, young Bart, we're going to give you a fighting chance.'

'You are? That's very decent of you,' the young man admitted.

'Heh! Heh!' Sam chuckled. 'We're not really though, are we Martha?'

'Shut up, Sam.'

'Sorry, Martha.'

'Now,' the old woman went on, 'we have measured out thirty paces and marked the spots with two table-cloths. The sheriff is standing on one. You can stand on the other.'

Bart looked at the table-cloth on the road just in front of him. 'Seems fair enough,' the young man shrugged. 'What happens then?' he asked.

'Then I count to three, you draw and fire,' Martha said.

'Uh huh. But what if I kill the old man?' Bart asked.

'Hah!' Martha cackled. 'Fat chance.'

'But I'm good,' Bart told her. 'I can hit a bottle at forty paces,' he boasted. 'With a bar-stool,' he added under his breath. The truth was he'd never fired his gun. For all he knew it was too rusted up to work.

'Sheriff Sam Simple is the best in the west,' Martha told him.

'He is?' Bart asked.

'I am?' the old man gasped.

'Once killed twenty men in the battle of the K.O. Corral,' Martha said fiercely.

'He did?' Bart frowned.

'I did?' Sam was shocked.

'And he only had one bullet!' Martha finished, getting quite carried away with her own story.

'In that case,' Bart told her, 'I think I should have some kind of help.'

'What kind?' Martha asked sharply.

'If you don't mind, I'll just do my fighting from behind this barrel,' Bart told her.

With a huge effort he picked up the barrel of powder and staggered towards the table-cloth on the ground.

He panted, struggled and wobbled. At last he reached the cloth. He placed one foot on it. Then two. He leaned forward to unload the barrel.

And vanished.

The part of the street where Bart had been standing was as empty as the Deadwood Hills where . . .

8

A Tiger and a Train

. . . Kate struggled wearily along the trail. Her high heeled boots were fine for dancing but hopeless for hurrying down hard roads. Her blue-spotted, cotton dress was too thin for the midnight air and she hugged Tiger to her to keep herself warm.

'Doesn't look like dawn yet,' she murmured to her cat. The cat didn't answer. 'We'll show those crooks,' she threatened. 'Hope old Sam roused a posse to help us.'

Kate stopped. 'Hey! It might all be over! We may have missed the action, Tiger. Shucks, I wanted to be in at the kill.'

Calamity Kate stomped on down the hill and soon reached the sign that said 'Deadwood Town – Population 365'.

'Hmm,' Kate said as she looked towards the lamplit streets. 'Bit too quiet.'

But when she reached the Copper Nugget Saloon she saw something which made her drop Tiger. The cat squawked and stalked off to explore the alleyways for mice and rats.

Kate tiptoed forward to look more closely at the sheriff and Martha who had clearly gone mad with the excitement.

They were on their hands and knees in the middle of the main street and had their heads stuck down one of the inspection covers for Deadwood's famous drains.

And, worse, old Sam Simple was shouting down the drain. 'OK, Big Bart, come out with your hands above your bed!'

Martha corrected him. 'Hands above your HEAD, Sam.'

'Er, hands above your bed pan!' Sam shouted.

'What on earth are you doing?' Kate asked.

Martha looked round sharply then her face softened as she recognised Calamity Kate. 'Oh, it's you, Kate! Good to see you made it all right. We've caught that Big Bart fella – the one who's planning to blow up our drains,' she said proudly.

'Drains?' Kate said weakly.

'That's right. Sam and me thought of the best plan in the world and it worked.'

'Drains?' Kate repeated.

'That's right. We challenged him to a duel. Told him he had to stand on a table-cloth to fight. 'Course, what Big Bart didn't know was that the table-cloth was placed over a drain inspection hole . . . and we'd taken the cover off! Went straight down – with his gunpowder – sharper than a bluebird's beak.'

'Drains?' Kate muttered stupidly.

'That's right,' said Sam, turning from his guarding duty at the hole. 'That'll teach those Flatfoot fellas to think they can damage our drains.'

Kate let out a scream of horror and panic. 'Nyaaaghh! Not DRAINS, Sheriff! Trains, I said. They're planning to rob the morning mail TRAIN!'

'Oh, dear,' the sheriff said.

'Oh, my,' Martha muttered. Then she brightened. 'Still, it was a good plan. He'll never rob a train while he's stuck in that drain.'

'Maybe not, but Sid the Kid can do anything while we hang around here,' Kate pointed out.

Martha's eyes narrowed. 'You mentioned something about this Sid the Kid earlier tonight.'

'That's right. He's the real leader. Big Bart is just his stooge,' Kate told her.

'But Sid the Kid died forty years ago,' Martha said.

'Looked alive enough to me,' Kate argued.

'He was hit by a runaway train as he tried to rob it,' Martha insisted.

'She could be right, Martha,' Sam cut in. 'That Bart fella looked too stupid to plan a robbery. Sid the Kid could easily be the brains behind an evil scheme like this, letting the Bart boy take all the risks. Seem to remember Sid was a bit of a coward.'

Martha sighed. 'OK, Sam. That means we've got to get the boy out of the drain, lock him up and get ourselves down to the station in time to catch the mail train.'

'All right, all right,' Sam moaned. 'Just remember, Martha Hepgutt, I'm the sheriff around here.'

'So, what do you suggest?' Martha asked patiently.

'I . . . er . . . suggest we get the kid out of the drain, lock him up and get ourselves down to the station.'

Martha gave him a smile as sweet as an acid drop and said, 'So, get him out.'

Sam turned to the deep, dark hole in the road and peered down to where . . .

. . . Big Bart had fallen heavily. Luckily the barrel had broken his fall and he'd landed on his head anyway, which was the thickest part of his body.

He straightened his hat and looked around. Some red powder spilled out of the barrel and into the trickle of dirty water. It foamed and fizzed into a pink cloud then drifted off down the drain.

A familiar voice laughed in the shadows. 'You really fell for that one, heh, heh, heh!'

Bart squinted up at Sid the Kid who leaned against the wall of the drain and grinned a grey grin.

Bart was cross. His temper was bubbling like the powder from the barrel. 'So this is where you've been hiding. This wasn't part of the plan.'

'No . . . but it could be,' Sid smiled.

'I have to get out of here first,' Bart complained. 'And as soon as I stick my head above the surface that sheriff'll just blast it clean off.'

'Hah! That sheriff couldn't hit a barn if he was standing inside it,' Sid the Kid drawled.

'The old lady . . .' Bart began.

'Lied,' Sid told him. 'She sure talks a good fight, but she can't fool Sid the Kid.'

'So, how do I get out?' Bart demanded.

'You don't – yet,' Sid told him.

'I'm not staying here,' Bart shuddered. 'It's smelly.'

'No, you're not staying here,' Sid agreed. 'You're going to the station and you're going underground all the way. They'll never be able to track us. We'll rob that train and be out of Deadwood before they know what's hit them. Now, get that barrel and roll it in front of you. I'll lead the way. These Deadwood drains go *everywhere* through this town. Wish we'd had hidden roads like this in my time,' Sid sighed.

'Your time?' Bart asked quickly.

'Yeh . . . when Billy and I used to rob banks . . . heck, I bet we could come back next week and blast clean through the bank floor. Make you the greatest robber of all time a trick like that.'

Bart was rolling the barrel, but still felt unhappy. 'If that girl tells them the plan they could still get to the station to stop us,' he reminded Sid.

Sid chuckled. 'We left that girl tied to the rail tighter than a rat to its tail,' he smirked.

But, of course . . .

9

Gunpowder Plot

. . . Kate stood at the edge of the drain inspection cover. 'Poor Bart could be knocked out cold,' she said looking down the empty drain. 'Might take hours for him to come round. We may be as well to leave him down there and see what's happening at the station.'

'Good thinking, Kate,' Martha said and led the way towards the far end of town. She didn't notice the fat, striped cat that followed them curiously.

As they walked Kate told Martha all she'd learned about the plan . . . and all she'd learned about Big Bart's bad boyhood. 'Lost his mother, eh?' Martha said. 'That's interesting. Very interesting. Explains a lot . . . a lot.'

'Like what?' Kate demanded, but Martha refused to answer.

The stationmaster was a young man with a thin worried face. As he listened to Martha's story his face became increasingly red and he fumbled with his tight collar. 'I'll trust you and the sheriff to sort it all out . . . the mail train is due in in five minutes. The banks' money is in the last carriage – with the guard in the brake van as usual. Good luck! Sorry I can't help you. It's my ten minute coffee-break.

I'll be back in two hours!' he added before he hurried back to his office and closed the door tight.

Kate, Sam and Martha moved out on to the platform. The morning air was slowly warming up and Martha breathed in deeply. Across the empty plain the horizon began to glow red with the coming sun and ragged black clouds drifted across it. A smudge of white smoke streamed over the grassland. 'Morning mail, dead on time,' Sam said half to himself.

Five minutes later the gleaming black engine roared and clanked into the station and squealed to a stop beside the Deadwood posse of three. Martha took charge and this time Sam didn't object – mainly because he had no idea what to do.

Martha dealt briskly with the guard in the brake van. 'Now, my man, the sheriff here wants you to take the Deadwood mail and go stay in the stationmaster's room for half an hour till this is all over.'

The man's sunburned face turned pale. 'But the carriage is full of fifty dollar bills – for the banks back East!' he argued.

'It will be safer in our hands than in yours,' Martha said sharply. 'Now do what I tell you – Sid the Kid is involved in this,' she warned.

'Sid the Kid,' the man laughed nervously. 'My dad told me about him. Wasn't he killed by a runaway train forty years ago?'

'Seems he's back robbing trains, just like in the old days. This young lady has seen him.'

'Sid the Kid?' the guard repeated weakly and scurried off to the safety of the station leaving the door to the brakevan open.

'What now?' Kate asked.

'Now?' Martha said. 'Now we climb inside the van and watch the windows. When Sid shows up we grab him!'

But Sid the Kid hadn't reached the station yet. At that moment . . .

. . . Sid the Kid was climbing from a drain hole just outside the railway shunting yards at Sagebush Junction half a mile away. Big Bart swung the barrel wearily up to the surface and groaned when he saw how far they were from the station.

'We'll never make it. Look! It's getting light. The train will leave at any moment.'

Sid's nose curled in a sneer. 'You forget you are talking to a great train robber. And you also forget my plan. You have to wait here with the powder – I'm going to send the van down the track to you, my little friend! Wait here!' he ordered. Sid the Kid slid behind an empty truck that was waiting in the yard and seemed to melt into the morning air.

'Ohh,' Bart moaned. 'They'll see him, they're sure to see him.'

But Sid the Kid must have reached the guard van without being seen. To Bart's amazement it began to trundle slowly down the line towards him. Sid was riding on the roof and grinning wickedly at his little partner. It rolled up to where Bart was sitting on his barrel and Sid screwed down the brake-wheel till it stopped. 'See! You didn't believe I could do it, did you?' he crowed and jumped to the ground.

'You haven't had time . . . ' Bart began to argue weakly.

Sid cut in, 'No time to argue. Roll that barrel under the van – that's right. Now, here's a fuse I took from the shop. It's old but it should work. Let's see,' Sid said as he measured a piece. 'That length should give us about four minutes to get clear before she blows.' Sid broke open the top of the barrel and stuck one end of the fuse in the red powder.

Bart grinned nervously. 'Then we just come back and pick up the fifty dollar bills?' he said.

Sid nodded and threw a match to the little man. 'Light this end and run,' he ordered.

Bart struck the match on the line and it flared and flickered in the morning air. He placed it against the end of the fuse and watched it smoulder. Slowly at first then with an eager fizz.

Bart looked around for Sid and he saw the gaunt, grey man at the door of the brake van, fiddling with a catch. 'Come on, Sid! What are you hanging round for?'

The thin villain grinned nastily. 'Just fastening the door on the outside,' he explained as he ran past Bart to the safe shelter of a line of wagons.

Bart turned to hurry after him. 'But *why?*' Bart persisted.

Sid stopped and sighed. 'Because the guard will notice that the brake van has moved – he'll jump out and pull the fuse from the barrel. The whole plot will be ruined!'

'Guard?' Bart gasped. 'There's a guard in that van?'

'Of course. You didn't think they'd leave all that money without a guard, did you?'

'He'll be hurt,' Bart cried. 'That wasn't part of the plan!'

'It was always part of *my* plan,' Sid smiled. 'And he won't be hurt – he won't feel a thing – he'll just be here in Dakota one minute and in four other states the next! Heh, heh, heh!'

But Bart wasn't listening. He was hurrying back across the tracks to the van where he thought a guard was in danger. In fact there wasn't a guard in the van at all. In the van . . .

10

The Train Trap

. . . Kate had been the first to spot that they were moving. 'Hey! The train's moving off. I guess Sid didn't make it after all.'

Martha squinted out of the window and said grimly, 'Maybe he did. Remember, his plan was to release this van and let it roll back to Sagebush Junction. You'll notice that's *just* the way we're headed.'

'How come we didn't see him uncouple this van?' Sheriff Sam Simple put in.

'How come we didn't see him in Deadwood?' Martha asked. 'He's craftier than a cartload of cats, that's how.'

'Ah, well,' Kate shrugged. 'I suppose we just wait till we reach Sagebush Junction. He'll have to climb in to blow the strong box – and that's when we grab him. Yeah?'

Martha nodded slowly but her face had a worried frown. 'I suppose so.'

'Nearly there,' Sam called out. 'And there's that little Bart character waiting with his barrel. Must have climbed out of the drain after all.'

'Don't forget,' Martha told him sternly. 'You say, "I arrest you in the name of the law".'

'Er . . . I arrest you in the name of my ma,' Sam muttered.

'Near enough,' Kate giggled. The thought of being so close to an arrest excited her. She held her breath and crouched down in a corner so the villains wouldn't see her when they stepped in. Then it would be too late. Sheriff Sam Simple would jump out . . . well, maybe ooze out . . . and grab them.

The van ground to a stop. Kate held her breath.

Kate went red in the face. She snatched another quick breath and held it again.

After five breaths the robbers had still not opened the door. Kate risked a peek through the window. 'Hey!' she hissed at Martha. 'That Bart's just running away!'

Then she gave a startled jump as she found herself looking into the colourless face of Sid the Kid. He leered at her with a twisted smile and reached for the catch beside the door. There was a sharp click before Sid turned and ran.

Kate tugged at the heavy door. 'They've locked us in!' she cried.

'Oh, no!' Martha cried. 'So much for my plans. Looks like they're going to get away with it after all.'

Kate sat on the floor. 'Just have to wait for the stationmaster and guard to turn up, I guess. Don't worry, Martha, at least we've saved the money.'

'Huh,' the old woman grunted and sat down next to Kate. 'Better sit down, Sam,' she called. 'Long wait.'

Then, through some joins in the thick wooden floor came the tingling smell of smoke.

Kate looked at Martha. 'Martha?'

'Yes, Kate?'

'Tell me that they would have to put the gunpowder in the van to blow the box. They would . . . wouldn't they?'

Martha winced. 'With that amount of gunpowder they wouldn't need to,' she said softly.

A tear filled Kate's eye as this sank in. 'I'd always hoped I'd get to Hollywood. Get to be a singing star or make it in the movies.'

Martha reached across and gripped her hand. 'I know, I know, my dear. But things are never as bad as they seem.'

Kate was just going to ask what Martha meant when the door flew open and Bart jumped into the van. He was almost speechless with panic.

'What are you doing here? You ain't the guard. Oh, never mind. You have to get out. This thing will blow up in three minutes. He turned back to the door. He looked out, turned pale and screamed. 'Ah! No!' and slammed the door. He put his back against it and stood there trembling and sweating.

'What's wrong?' Kate asked.

'Out there!'

'What's out there?'

'Cat! Striped cat! I hate them!'

'Well stay in here and it can't get you. But if you don't mind we'd like to get out before we blow up in two and a half minutes time.'

Kate marched to the door, muttering, 'Probably just my Tiger come to see where his breakfast is,' she pushed the trembling Bart aside and reached for the door handle. And as she did so she heard that click again.

Even her freckles had turned pale as she turned back to the others and announced, 'I think that Sid just locked us all in.'

'Hey!' Sam Simple said suddenly. 'You're that crook fella ain't you? I – er – arrest you in the name of your ma!'

'I ain't got a ma,' Bart muttered miserably. 'Looks like I never will now,' he sighed.

'Sad that,' Martha said calmly. 'Same as I never really had a son. Leastways I *did* have a son . . . but I lost him.'

For a moment Kate forgot that she had just two minutes to live. 'You lost your son, Martha? That's terrible! How did it happen?'

'Oh, I went out with Josiah for a picnic in the hills above Flatfoot . . . '

Bart licked his lips and looked at her. 'How long ago?' he asked.

Martha looked hard at the young man. 'Oh, twenty-something years ago.'

'Twenty-three and a half years?' he asked excitedly.

Martha nodded. 'That's right. Twenty-three and a half years exactly. Josiah went to get wood for a fire . . . I fell asleep in the hot sun. Woke up half an hour later and he was gone.'

Big Bart's lip trembled. He raised his arms. 'Ma!' he said simply.

Martha looked at him hard. 'No! If my son had

lived he wouldn't have grown up to be some no good crook.'

Tears filled Bart's eyes. 'And if I'd had a mother to care for me I would never have been led astray by a rat like Sid the Kid,' he sighed.

'You know, I do believe you're right,' Martha smiled and put an arm around the little man.

'Oh, ' Kate sniffed. 'That's the saddest thing I ever saw in my life.'

Bart looked up through his red-rimmed eyes. 'Sad? I found my mother after searching all my life.'

'Ah,' Kate nodded. 'But you found her at the END of your life. With just fifteen seconds to go before you're both blown into tiny pieces.'

'Ten seconds,' Martha corrected her.

'Nine,' Kate nodded.

'Eight,' Martha said.

'Seven . . . '

'Six . . . '

II

Runaway Train – Again

' . . . five,' Sid the Kid chuckled. He waited behind the empty trucks with his fingers stuck in his ears.

That's why he didn't hear the train coming.

' . . . four . . . '

The trouble was that no one had told the driver that his guard was in the stationmaster's room.

He looked at his pocket watch and reckoned that the train should be leaving. Then he looked for the guard and saw that the brake van had run down the hill.

'Guess I'd better fetch it,' he told his fireman. 'Full of money. Can't afford to lose that!' and he put the train into reverse and set off down the hill.

That gave the signalman a shock. He saw the train sliding back towards the rail yards at Sagebush Junction. It was going to collide with the empty trucks and cause a huge wreck. Thinking quicker than a humming-bird's wing he switched the points to send the train on to an empty track.

He wiped his brow with a red spotted handkerchief. He felt quite pleased with himself . . . until he looked down that empty track and saw a thin, grey man run on to the line, crouch down and stick his fingers in his ears.

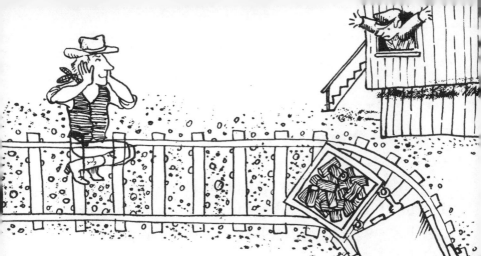

'Get off the line!' he screamed from his box. But the stupid man couldn't hear because he had his fingers in his ears.

The driver looked back from his cab. 'Dang points!' he cursed. 'We're on the wrong track!'

'Stop the train,' he ordered the fireman.

'That'll be hard,' the fireman chuckled. 'The brake van is down at Sagebush Junction!'

'Dang! Dang! Dang!' the driver swore as the train picked up speed.

That was when the driver spotted the thin, grey man run on to the track and crouch down with his fingers in his ears.

'Blow the whistle!' he cried.

The train whistle howled. The thin, grey man couldn't hear it because he had his fingers in his ears.

'We're going to hit him in four seconds,' the driver screamed above the screeching steam.

'Funny,' the fireman laughed. 'Same thing happened forty years ago to a train robber by the name of . . . '

*   *   *

' . . . three . . . ' Sid the Kid counted. Then he looked up.

A pained look flashed over his face just before the train hit him. And, if anyone had been able to hear him, they'd have heard him say, 'Oh, no. Not *again*!'

As the rushing, screeching train hit him he was looking towards the brake van with that load of lovely money and four people who were counting . . .

*   *   *

' . . . two . . . one . . . '

Three of them closed their eyes and clenched their fists tight. All except Martha Hepgutt who smiled gently as she wrapped an arm tightly round little Bart's shoulder.

'Nothing!' Kate said simply.

And that was true.

Nothing.

Absolutely nothing happened.

The smoke that had been creeping through the floorboards drifted away. Kate looked at Martha and waited.

'Bart,' Martha said. 'Did you ever go to school?'

The young man shook his head. 'They always picked on me because of my size – so I stayed away.'

'If you'd had parents it might have been different,' Martha said. 'I guess you never learned to read?'

He shook his head. 'Not really.'

'Thought so. I couldn't help noticing that barrel you had in the street,' she said.

'The gunpowder?' Bart asked.

'Yes,' said Martha. 'I guess that, if you could read, you'd have known what was really in that barrel.'

'Not gunpowder?' Kate asked.

'Not gunpowder?' Bart laughed. 'But it was red powder, and Sid said . . . '

'I guess Sid can't read either. No, Bart, what the label on the side of the barrel said was "Sherbet". When Josiah and I had a shop in Flatfoot we sold it from the barrel just like that.'

Kate sank to the floor in happy relief. 'I'll eat the whole barrel when I get out of here. When . . . '

Barman Bart

. . . the stationmaster opened the van about half an hour later, four weary but happy people stepped out into the brilliant early sunshine.

'About time,' Sheriff Sam Simple complained.

'Sorry, sir,' the young man said, choking on his tight collar. 'We had to catch the train first . . . then the driver reported an accident. Said he ran over a fella at thirty miles an hour. We had to search the tracks for the body. We found . . . '

'Nothing,' Martha said wisely.

The stationmaster blinked. 'How did you know?'

The old woman shrugged. 'Because Sid the Kid died forty years ago – run over by a train – and you can't kill a ghost.'

'Will we see him again?' Bart asked nervously.

'I think if I'd had a shock like he's just had I wouldn't be hanging around for more!' Martha chuckled. 'I reckon we should all go for a glass of sarsaparilla at . . .'

★   ★   ★

. . . The Copper Nugget Saloon.

Sam supped a sarsaparilla. Slowly. Sam did everything slowly these days. But there was a sparkle of life in his eyes that wasn't there the night before.

Martha sat at the table with Kate while Bart worked busily tidying up the bar-room.

'Looks like you've lost your job, Martha,' Sam chuckled.

'Time I retired and handed the business over to a younger person.'

'To your son,' Kate added eagerly.

Martha blushed and looked at the floor.

Sam looked at her carefully. Bart, the new barman, had stepped outside to paint the door with fresh green paint so there was no chance of him overhearing the conversation. 'Never knew you had a son, Martha.'

'Oh yes,' Kate chirped. 'But she lost him twenty-three years ago, didn't you, Martha?'

Martha looked up at her sheepishly. 'No, Kate.'

Kate gasped.

Sheriff Sam Simple nodded wisely. 'Told a little white lie, eh, Martha?'

Martha nodded. 'When Kate told me Bart's story I had to feel sorry for him. So I told that story about losing a son.'

'You said you were his mother,' Kate blinked.

'No-o,' Sam said slowly. 'Bart said that. Martha just didn't argue. And where's the harm. The boy's happy. The railroad company and the bank are happy. Everybody's happy.'

'Except me,' Kate sighed. 'That thieving Sid stole my savings! I'll never get to Hollywood.'

'You'll make plenty of money singing in bars – a talented girl like you!' Sam smiled.

It was Kate's turn to blush. Sam knew, just as Martha knew, that sometimes a little white lie that makes someone happy is forgivable.

Kate hurried outside to tell Barman Bart that the Sheriff said she was a talented singer.

Bart didn't remind Kate that Sheriff Sam Simple was as deaf as the doorpost he was painting . . . Sam couldn't tell a songbird from a train whistle.

Bart was learning kindness too. He looked proudly at the saloon and whistled an old tune.

He didn't know the words . . . but, for once Kate did.

'Mid pleasures and palaces, though we may roam,' she sang and Bart joined in.

Together they finished at the tops of their very loud voices, 'There's no place like home!'